The Stick and Mr. Pig

Pick ONE 1 2

① The Case of the Missing Marbles

Story by Daniel Hobart

For my mom and dad who love the real life Stick and Pig.

Art by Julie Heide

For my amazing family, Matt, Mitchell, Griffin, Marin and our boss, Eileen.

Draw Everyday!
Julie Heide

Always pet your pets!

HeideHo LLC
©Copyright 2018
Available on Kindle and online stores
Printed by CreateSpace, An Amazon.com Company

"They're always late! We have customers waiting!"

Across the field
and into the woods...

"You're late!
Did you at least bring
your paperwork from
yesterday?" Eileen barked!

"Uh… the dog
ate our paperwork!"
said Mr. Pig

ha!

ha!   Ha!

"What!? You ARE dogs!"
Eileen barked louder!

"Just kidding, Boss!
We brought it,"
smiled The Stick.

"Get changed for work!
We have customers waiting,"
Eileen barked.

6

"Good morning, Ms. Badger, what
can we help you with today?"
The Stick inquired.

"You can call me Helen,
and I've lost my glasses!
I can't find them anywhere!
I can't see without them!"

"Laughing?
Why are you laughing?
This isn't funny.
I should report you
to your supervisor!"
Helen exclaimed.

Ha, ha!

Ha,
Ha,
Ha!

Hee, hee,
woof!

Ha, Ha, Ha!

Ruff Ruff!

The Stick reached through the window, and
s - l - o - w - l - y
pushed Helen's glasses back onto her nose.

Helen's eyes got really big in her glasses.
She started laughing.
Even Eileen laughed, but just a little.

The Stick and Mr. Pig
turned back to the counter.

All they saw was a **really BIG** grey blob!

Then all of a sudden, the really BIG grey blob turned into
a really BIG Blue EYE!

The **really big** blue eye turned into a GIANT TRUNK and reached through the window.

The Stick **dodged,** but it **grabbed** Mr. Pig!

"Whoa! I didn't even know
we had elephants around here!
What can we do for you?"
asked Mr. Pig.

"I'm Tiny! And I've lost my
marbles!" he groaned.

"Oh No! Where were your marbles, when you saw them last?" The Stick inquired.

"They were In a bag, in my tent!" Tiny answered.

Bag

"You live in a tent?" The Stick asked.

"Yeah, I worked for the circus. It's a pretty big tent. Plus I have wi-fi," Tiny replied.

"We need to check your tent.
Mind giving us a ride?"
the detectives asked.

"You got it!
Hop on!"

Tiny paraded the pet detectives
through the wild woods,
across a rushing river,

Wheeeeeeeee!!!!

into a fiery field,
   down a steep slope,
      and finally to his tent.

"Ok, Tiny, please walk us through what happened," asked Mr. Pig.

"I'm always hungry when I wake up, so I eat right away," replied Tiny.

"Then I grab my bag of marbles, go outside and play. But they went missing this morning!"

The ace pet detectives headed
outside and sniffed around.

Almost immediately,
Mr. Pig picked up a scent.

Mr. Pig followed the scent into the tall grass. He pointed and...

The Stick ran full speed and closed in on the culprit.

The Stick mumbled, his mouth full of the suspect mouse.

Got 'em

"What's your name, mouse?"
Mr. Pig demanded

I'm Zeus!

"Please empty the bag."
Mr. Pig directed.

My Marbles !

On the next page,

Pick ONE pawprint to pick your ending!

"I'm sorry."

Pick ONE 1 2

"I watched him playing with these marbles everyday and it looked fun. But I was scared of him, because he was really big. So, I stole them this morning to play with them. I'm sorry."

If this is your answer, turn to page 32.

30

"Don't you know that it's **wrong** to take someone else's property?" The Stick asked.

"Yes, I knew it was wrong. I made a very bad choice. I'm very sorry I took your marbles." Zeus cried.

"Are you **sorry** because you got **caught**? or because **stealing** is wrong?" The Stick inquired.

"Because stealing is wrong. Those are your marbles, and I need to respect that," Zeus sulked.

friends

kites

CONCLUSION

TURN to page 40 for the conclusion.

"So, your story, is that you did not steal the marbles?" Mr. Pig started the interrogation.

"I followed your scent all the way from this tent into the field where The Stick caught you!"

"We also found you holding Tiny's bag of marbles."
The Stick added.

"Interesting... A piece of cheese in the marble bag, We'll send that to the crime lab for testing ASAP!"

"Admit it, you took the marbles."
Mr. Pig declared.

"OKAY, so I took the marbles.
What's the big deal?"
Zeus shrugged.

"You're guilty and you lied.
Now you're going to jail!"
Mr. Pig exclaimed.

The Stick nodded at Mr. Pig.
as they rummaged for sticks and brush.

The pet detectives quickly fashioned the
materials into a mini mouse jail.

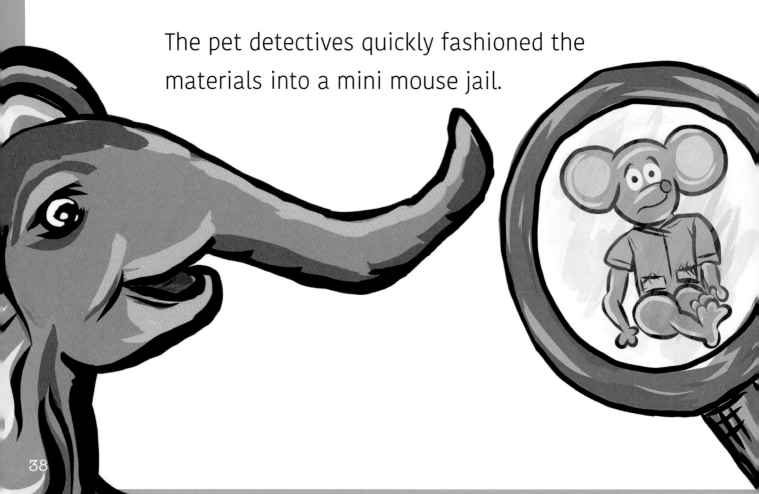

The Stick and Mr. Pig met Eileen back at HQ.

"You two took so long I had to send everyone else home," Eileen barked.

"Well, we did solve the case of the missing marbles!" Mr. Pig reported.

"Anything happen
while we were gone?"
The Stick inquired.

"A lot of the animals in
line today said the fleas
were really bad this year."

"We need to
keep an eye out,"
Eileen barked.

Join us next time for

Pick ONE 1 2

② The Case of the Tipping Trash Cans

Let's talk about...

The Stick and Mr. Pig

① The Case
of the
Missing
Marbles

① What did Zeus do wrong to be thrown into mouse jail?

② What did you think about the consequences of his actions, was it fair?

③ What emotions do you think Zeus felt when Tiny forgave him for taking the marbles?

④ Can you think of a time you felt like Tiny or Zeus?

⑤ Did you ever take something that wasn't yours? Were you scared you would get caught? Was it worth it?

When you are **stuck** in the spotlight, like Zeus, **YOU have a BIG CHOICE...**

After all, isn't HONESTY always the best policy?

45

The Stick and Mr. Pig

Based on THE REAL life pets...

The Stick

The Stick is a whippet which is just about a half-size greyhound. Whippets are sighthounds, so they will chase anything that runs from them. Whippets are especially fast, in fact, they are the fastest accelerating dog and can run up to 35 mph. The Stick's real name is Yoda, and Daniel got him in 2004. While he's not as fast or agile as he used to be, he is even more sweet and kind. And remember, always cover up your whippet with a blanket when they sleep. Or else.

Mr. Pig

Mr. Pig is a short-legged, nose-to-the-ground, mutt. Most likely he is part beagle and basset hound, and some other stuff. His name is Percy and he was rescued by Daniel's parents from a home that wasn't very good for pets. It took several years for Percy to warm up to people, and it was clear that he had been abused. Everyone thinks he's about 8 years old because he's getting some white hair on his muzzle. He is the cuddliest little guy now. But, he'll eat anything. Socks. Dish towels. Underwear.

Eileen

Eileen's name is actually Eileen. She's an adorable and sweet Boston Terrier. Miss Eileen is truly the boss of the Heide family. She snores louder than a train, snorts rather than barks, and naps whenever possible. Rescued from a shelter at age 10, after losing her owner, she came to her forever home with 3 teeth and one bad knee. Eileen wants to remind you to rescue pets without homes. Every sweet doggie deserves a cozy warm bed to nap in... and someone to boss around.

www.Heideho.org

Written and Illustrated by REAL life humans...

Daniel Hobart

Daniel is a trial lawyer. You might not realize it, but trial lawyers are story-tellers. A couple years ago he started making books for his younger cousins. Having bribed Julie with various and asundry things (an iPad Pro), she began to illustrate his books. A year later, HeideHo was born with the first book series, The Stick and Mr. Pig. This series is really for his parents, who take care of both Yoda and Percy. They're all sharing retirement, with long naps (on the bed) and short walks. Always pet your pets!

Julie Heide

Julie has been an artist for her whole life. As a graphic designer, elementary art teacher, private art lesson instructor, grad student, wife, mom, and friend... she has a LOT going on. Stick and Pig captured her heart and illustrating became her next passion. With endless ideas and inspiration, Julie loves painting, sculpting and any form of creating she can get her hands on. You never know what she will be making next!

Made in the USA
Lexington, KY
18 May 2018